POPPY'S FIRST YEAR

SUSAN WILLIAMS

Four Winds Press New York

For Ros

First American Edition 1989   Printed in Portugal by Printer Portuguesa
10 9 8 7 6 5 4 3 2 1
Library of Congress Cataloging-in-Publication Data. Williams, Susan, date. Poppy's
first year/by Susan Williams.—1st American ed.   p.   cm. Summary: During
baby Poppy's first year, brother Sam is sometimes impatient, but usually proud.
ISBN 0-02-793031-9
[1. Babies—Fiction. 2. Brothers and sisters—Fiction.]
I. Title. PZ7.W66818Po   1989   [E]—dc19   88-21345   CIP   AC

Sam's new brother or sister will
be born soon.

Mom's tummy gets bigger as the baby grows inside her. Everyone helps to make the baby's room ready, and Sam helps Mom bring out the cradle that he slept in when he was tiny. They talk a lot about the baby's coming.

"Sam," Mom says one morning, "I think the baby's going to come today. Gran will look after you while Dad and I are away at the hospital."

Before they leave, Mom gives Sam a big hug and a kiss. "See you soon," she calls from the car window, and waves. "See you soon," Sam and Gran call, waving back.

Not long after Mom and Dad arrive at the hospital, the baby is born.

Her face is purplish red and wrinkled, and she's got lots of black spiky hair. She cries loudly. Mom holds her close, and she and Dad gaze at their new baby. They think she's beautiful.

"We'll call her Poppy," Mom says.

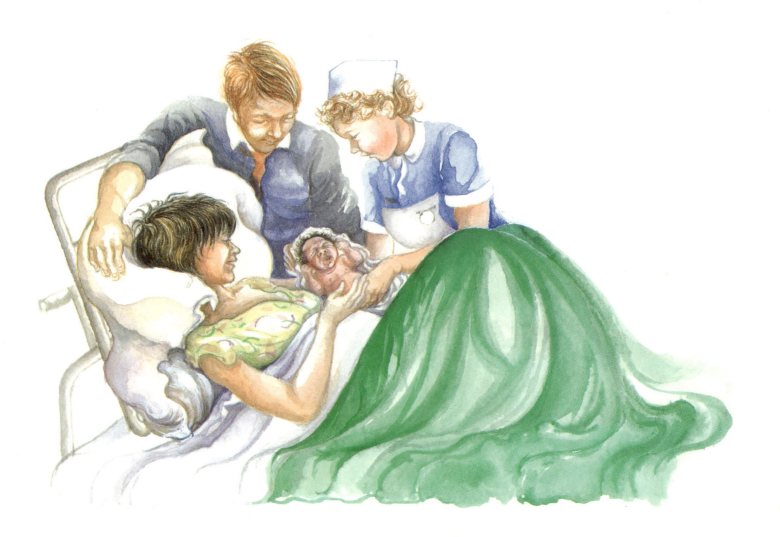

Later a nurse weighs the baby and measures her. She writes Poppy's name on four pink plastic tapes and puts them around her wrists and ankles so that she won't be mixed up with any of the other newborn babies. The nurse carefully feels Poppy's "soft spot" on top of her head, takes her temperature, and listens to her heartbeat.

When Dad gets home with the news about Poppy, Sam and Gran are having dinner.
"It's a girl!" says Dad. Sam is very excited and can hardly wait for the next day to come, when he can see Mom and Poppy. Before he goes to bed, he makes a card for Mom and wraps up a present he's chosen especially for the baby.

When he sees Poppy for the first time, she's lying asleep in her crib by Mom's bed.
Then she wakes and cries, so Gran holds her and soothes her.

Sam strokes her warm pink fist, which curls tightly around one of his fingers. He's surprised how strong she is.

Mom thinks Sam's card is better than any you can buy. She unwraps his present for Poppy, a soft toy dog with a jingling bell in its tummy.

"She'll love that, Sam," Mom says.

At first when they are home, Poppy cries a great deal and Mom has to feed her often.
In between feedings, she sleeps, sometimes just for a few minutes, sometimes for hours.

Sam and Dad take turns cuddling her. They hold her carefully because her neck isn't strong enough yet to support her head.

In a few weeks, Poppy makes little sighs and squeaks of contentment when she's being fed and changed. Now she really looks at Sam and smiles at him.
If they're out for a walk, Poppy lies on her back and looks up at the shapes of branches, leaves, and rooftops against the sky.

"Look, Hannah, here's my new sister," Sam says proudly to his friend when they meet her coming home from play group with her big sister.

Poppy's hands and fingers are her first toys. From the age of two months, she spends a lot of time watching them moving and trying to bring them to her mouth.

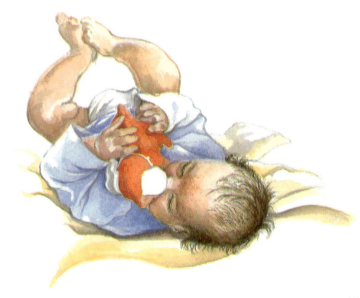

Now she's awake much more. She learns to use her hands to touch, hold, and taste all sorts of things. It's her way of finding out about them.

Poppy's neck gets stronger, too. By the time she's three months old, she's lying on her tummy and trying to lift her head up to see everything that's going on. Not every baby is the same, but Poppy can soon prop herself up and peer over the edge of the carriage, gurgling and cooing to anyone who stops to chat.

Mom usually reads Sam a story
when she's feeding Poppy.
Now that she's older, Poppy is
curious about the rustling pages
and bright colors of the book.
She tries to grab it. "No,
Poppy," says Sam crossly,
"that's MY book."

The time comes when Mom's milk isn't enough food for Poppy any longer. But she doesn't like strained carrots or mashed bananas much when she tastes them for the first time. She spits them out!

When she's six months old, a tiny white tooth appears in her bottom gum. Soon after, there's one next to it. Now she can chew toast crusts and enjoy the same food as the rest of the family — but Mom still mashes it up.
Sometimes Sam helps to feed her, and Poppy thinks that's good.

Summer is coming and Poppy
lies on a rug in the garden,
raising her head and shoulders.
She's getting ready to crawl.
She tucks her legs under her
tummy and rocks backward
and forward, trying to reach
the purple ring.

Now when Mom reads to Sam, Poppy happily sits beside them, looking at books or playing with her toys.

Poppy is nearly eight months old when she starts to crawl.
She races all over the house, exploring everywhere.

About the same time, she
learns to pull herself up so she
can stand. She's tall enough to
reach all sorts of forbidden
things. She opens cupboards,
rummages along shelves, and
plays with anything she
likes the look of.

Now Sam must remember to hide away his special toys and books.

Poppy and Sam love the beach. Poppy stares at the wide
expanse of sea and sky and at other children playing games on
the sand or in the sea. She laughs and kicks her fat little legs
when she lies splashing in a sandy pool.

Sam is good at building sand castles and thinks his is the best on the beach!

Poppy likes picking up pebbles and shells and dropping them into her bucket. Mom and Dad have to watch her carefully to make sure she doesn't swallow any.

Something special happens when Poppy is ten months old.
Mom moves her crib into Sam's room.

She isn't just gurgling and cooing now, but trying out all sorts of sounds and a few real words. So Sam understands quite a lot that Poppy says to him.

Early in the morning, they shout and giggle at each other. Poppy throws all her toys out of her crib, one by one. She bounces up and down with shrieks of excitement, waiting for Sam to throw them back.

It's fun, too, when Poppy and Sam share the bath.
Poppy doesn't wreck Sam's toys so often, now that she's nearly
eleven months old. But Sam still gets very cross when he finds
her playing with special toys he thinks he's hidden away.
She can pick up small, delicate things quite carefully and turn
pages in a book — though she sometimes tears them!

When Sam goes to play group, Poppy comes with Mom, although she's much too small to join. But she loves playing with Sam and his friends in the big cardboard-box house, or shaking the maracas and bells when they all have a sing-along.

Today is Poppy's birthday. She's one year old! She can just stagger along on her feet if she's holding on to something, and it won't be long before she takes her very first steps alone. Mom and Dad have given her a lamb on wheels to push.

Sam gets impatient because Poppy takes such a long time to unwrap her presents. She likes the boxes and the wrapping paper as much as the things inside.
Sam's present is a bag of colored blocks, and he builds her a high, wobbly tower. "Come on, Poppy, knock them down!" he says.